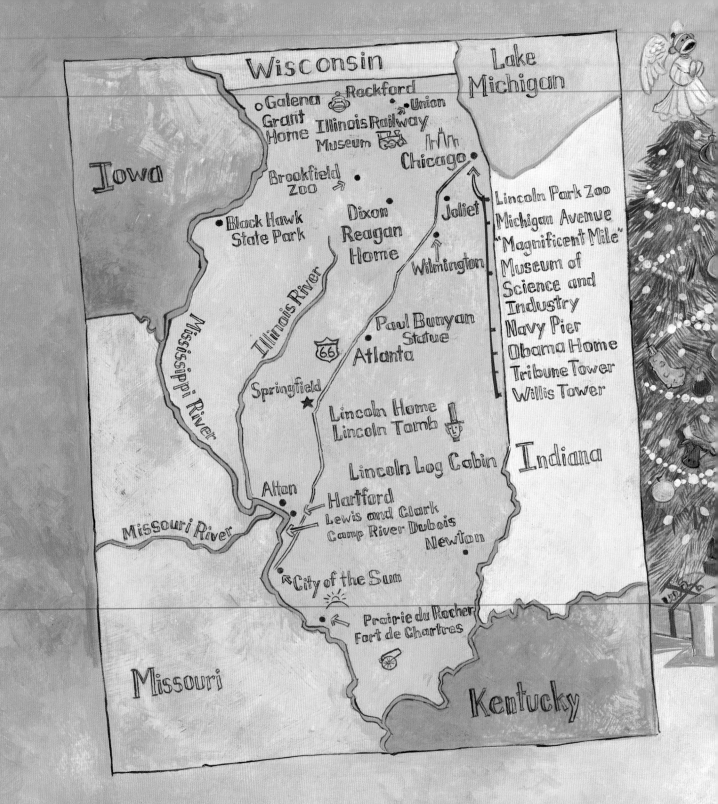

Wisconsin

Lake Michigan

Iowa

Galena
Grant Home
Rockford
Union
Illinois Railway Museum
Brookfield Zoo
Chicago

Black Hawk State Park
Dixon
Reagan Home
Joliet
Wilmington

Illinois River

Paul Bunyan Statue
66
Atlanta

Springfield
Lincoln Home
Lincoln Tomb

Lincoln Log Cabin

Indiana

Mississippi River

Alton
Hartford
Lewis and Clark
Camp River Dubois
Newton

Missouri River

City of the Sun

Prairie du Rocher
Fort de Chartres

Missouri

Kentucky

Lincoln Park Zoo
Michigan Avenue
"Magnificent Mile"
Museum of
Science and
Industry
Navy Pier
Obama Home
Tribune Tower
Willis Tower

The Twelve Days of Christmas in Illinois

written by
Gina Bellisario

illustrated by
Jeffrey Ebbeler

STERLING CHILDREN'S BOOKS
New York

Hi, Mia!

It was hard, but I _finally_ got Mom and Dad to spill the beans about your Christmas surprise. They said you're spending 12 whole days in Illinois . . . with us! Thanks for being a really cool gift—does that mean you'll come wrapped in glittery paper? Better wear a warm coat, too, because Midwest winters are **COLD**. You can practically ice-skate on our driveway, and Dad said snow is on the way. But the weather is just part of what makes my state great. You'll see the other reasons when you arrive. They're _my_ gifts to _you_!

From ghosts that boo-hoo to "cheezborgers," Illinois has it all. There are mighty rivers, monster men, a whole lot of monkey business, and some seriously **TALL** towers. Have you ever stood above the clouds? If you haven't, just wait.

So get packing, but leave extra room for the gifts. Borrow your dad's suitcase. The big one, okay?

Bear hugs from your favorite cousin,

Sam

Dear Mom and Dad,

Here I am in chilly Illinois! Lots of icy snow here—almost two feet. From the bus stop, Uncle Joe, Aunt Mary, and Sam shouted, "Welcome to the Prairie State!" Prairie State? I wondered. <u>Where?</u> Maybe it's under all this snow. . . .

At their house, Uncle Joe fixed me a secret snack. He didn't want me to peek while he was getting it ready, so Sam and I walked out to their backyard prairie. Sam said that when it's warm, more than 100 kinds of grasses and wildflowers grow, some with roots 11 feet deep! Thanks to all those plants, prairies make GREAT butterfly homes. Monarch butterflies love it here in spring and summer. But before winter comes, they're off to sunny Mexico!

When Uncle Joe called, "Snack time!" we ran for the door and guess what? I saw a ruby red cardinal, the state bird! There it was, next to the house, sitting cozy in the state tree, a branchy white oak. Uncle Joe said that white oak wood makes the best root beer barrels. Then he handed me a giant root beer float and a bowl of popcorn—the state snack! I shared some with Ruby, my new beautiful birdie.

Love,
Mia

On the first day of Christmas,
my cousin gave to me . . .

a cardinal
in a white oak tree.

Dear Mom and Dad,

Hip, hip, hurrah! Today we set off for Camp River Dubois near Alton. The brave U.S. explorers Meriwether Lewis and William Clark launched their important voyage from this spot. Sam and I could imagine exactly how they would have looked in their incredible 55-foot keelboat.

Over 200 years ago, President Thomas Jefferson asked them to chart the unknown West. Would they see volcanoes? Woolly mammoths? Jefferson thought so. Instead, their Corps of Discovery (that was the fancy name for their team) found 300 new animal and plant species AND the Rocky Mountains! They drew EVERYTHING in their journals. Lewis even blazed their trail, marking land with his branding iron.

Next we headed to the "City of the Sun." Aunt Mary told us that around 700 A.D., prehistoric natives called Cahokians settled near Collinsville and built a city with 120 HUGE grassy mounds. Nearby, tree-size posts stood tall, placed in a circle. Experts think the natives used Woodhenge (that's the fancy name for the circle) to mark the seasons or special festivals. As for Ruby? She thought one post made a terrific perch. (Or maybe she was just pooped from our adventures!)

Onward, voyagers!
Mia

On the second day of Christmas,
my cousin gave to me . . .

2 voyagers

and a cardinal in a white oak tree.

Cover your ears, Mom and Dad! BOOM!

   This morning, we soldiered on to Prairie du Rocher, a town founded by French colonists. Until the 1760s, Illinois was part of a country called New France! The town's Fort de Chartres—an old French trading post—is stone-cold proof.

   Colonists traded a LOT at the fort. They swapped things like bear's oil (ew!) and tongues (double ew!). Thousands of people still celebrate French trade at the fort's annual Rendezvous. When Sam went last June, he saw tepees and rope makers, but his favorite part was the opening parade. The sound of drums and fifes filled the air, and EVERYONE was dressed like a French soldier—even Uncle Joe! Sam heard a cannon fire, too. He says his ears are STILL ringing!

   At bedtime Sam told me a super spooky story about a quieter parade at Fort de Chartres. Sometimes, around midnight, people swear they see a line of 40 horse-drawn wagons, foot soldiers, weeping ladies, and one casket appear from the fort. Wheels pound the road. Horses kick up dust. All. Totally. Silent.

   How do you say BOO in French?

                                         Love,
                                         Mia

On the third day of Christmas,
my cousin gave to me . . .

3 gray ghosts

2 voyagers,
and a cardinal in a white oak tree

Dear Mom and Dad,

Uncle Joe told us a goofy joke today. What does a river say when it runs into another river? Just going with the flow. HA!

This morning we rolled into a river town called Hartford. Uncle Joe didn't want us to miss a VERY important meeting—the Meeting of the Great Rivers! Here, the Mississippi, the Missouri, and the Illinois rivers all join together. Waaay up in the Lewis and Clark Confluence Tower (named after the explorers), Sam and I could see the Missouri empty into the others. Eeew . . . that river needs a bath! Sam said lots of dirt and sand ride on the Missouri. It's even been nicknamed "Big Muddy."

Did you know the name Mississippi means Big River? The Mighty Miss is America's largest waterway. It runs through TEN states. Things like paper and corn are shipped on its current, cutting down on highway pollution. One barge can carry the same load as 75 trucks!

Oh, I almost forgot. From our birdie-eyed view, we also saw BALD EAGLES! They like the cold Mississippi water since it's full of fish. Maybe that's why Illinois has a huge bald eagle population.

Your Mighty Miss,
Mia

GREAT RIVER ROAD
ILLINOIS

MEETING OF THE
GREAT RIVERS

On the fourth day of Christmas,
my cousin gave to me . . .

4 soaring birds

3 gray ghosts, **2** voyagers,
and a cardinal in a white oak tree.

Let's play a name game, Mom and Dad!

Which nickname belonged to our 16th president? Was it "Father Abraham," "Rail Splitter," or "Ancient One"? If you guessed "all three," you're right! (His neighbors also called him Abe. Honest.)

Today we visited Springfield—the state's capital and the much-loved home of guess-who. When Lincoln first arrived here, he had no money. He even rode in on a borrowed horse. What he _did_ have were the best stories EVER! "The Great Story Teller" (neighbors called him that, too) made crowds crack up.

Next to his funny bone was a soft spot for animals. Lincoln wouldn't hunt deer like people did in those days and probably didn't care if they snacked on his vegetable garden. (Aunt Mary sometimes finds white-tailed deer at dusk, eating her potatoes. Yep, she cares . . . a LOT!)

The word Illinois means Tribe of Superior Men. Superior is right! Not only is Illinois the Land of Lincoln, it's the land of three other U.S. presidents—Ulysses S. Grant, Ronald Reagan, and Barack Obama.

Just call me your Illinois tour guide,

Mia

P.S. Before we said bye to Abe, Sam promised me a super-sized surprise! Can't wait!

On the fifth day of Christmas,
my cousin gave to me . . .

5 golden deer

4 soaring birds, 3 gray ghosts, 2 voyagers,
and a cardinal in a white oak tree.

Whoa.

Sam's surprise really <u>was</u> a SUPER size. As we left Springfield, he pointed out a statue of young Abe, the rail splitter. It was as tall as a tree! (I knew Lincoln was the tallest president in U.S. history, but wow!) Next we cruised onto the "Main Street of America," historic Route 66 (now Interstate 55). It was the first major highway connecting big cities to small towns. Tons of stores sat roadside, and they all wanted attention. Bring in the GIANTS! Enormous ads appeared on buildings and garage doors. Even barns! Big statues sold stuff, too, and still do. Sam's favorites are the Pink Elephant, the Joliet Jackhammer, the Gemini Giant, and the Sinclair Dinosaur.

Sam was hungry, so Uncle Joe pulled up to a 19-foot-tall statue of Paul Bunyan . . . holding a mega-HUGE hotdog! At a diner, I ordered a corn dog (some say it was invented in Illinois). Sam got the local specialty—a horseshoe sandwich. It's made of toast, ham, and french fries, covered in gooey cheese. Mmm . . .

Motorin' on,
Mia

HISTORIC

ILLINOIS
US
66

ROUTE

1926-30

On the sixth day of Christmas, my cousin gave to me . . .

6 roadside giants

5 golden deer, 4 soaring birds, 3 gray ghosts, 2 voyagers, and a cardinal in a white oak tree.

Dear Mom and Dad,

Ever walked in a Native American's footsteps? I did. They belonged to a Sauk leader: Ma-ka-tai-me-she-kia-kiak. Black Hawk, for short.

Today we took about a jillion steps around Black Hawk State Park. The Sauk and Meskwaki nations must have, too. They lived here for almost 100 years! In the park's museum, Sam and I saw dioramas of the tribes making candy from maple syrup, plus a rare dugout canoe that some kids found.

Sam wanted to find an arrowhead, but our hike was turning my toes into icicles, so our guide helped us make a campfire. Then Sam got a toastier idea: S'MORES!

We ate gooey marshmallows as our guide talked about Black Hawk. He was a warrior—born into the Thunder clan—and led large war parties to victory. But he was tricked into signing peace papers that gave away Sauk land to the U.S. government. After Black Hawk realized what had happened, he and 1,500 followers fought back for their home. Known as The Black Hawk War, the fight lasted for 15 weeks and was lost at the Battle of Bad Axe.

Love,
Mia

On the seventh day of Christmas,
my cousin gave to me . . .

7 s'mores a-melting

6 roadside giants, 5 golden deer,
4 soaring birds, 3 gray ghosts, 2 voyagers,
and a cardinal in a white oak tree.

GRAHAM
CRACKERS

MARSHMALLOW

Quick, Mom and Dad. Call the doctor . . .

I've got Sock Monkey MADNESS! Today we went to Rockford, home of the wacky plush primate.

Swedish immigrant John Nelson started the craze. In the 1800s, he built The Nelson Knitting Company, maker of the original Rockford Red Heel. Farmers used the socks to keep their feet warm, but a group of creative nuns came up with a cuddlier idea: they turned them into Christmas toys, and sock monkeys were born. Every year, Rockford goes ape at the Sock Monkey Madness Festival. There are make-your-own-monkey classes and even a "Miss Sockford" pageant. (Sam is planning to enter his yodeling "Hairy" Potter sock monkey. Cross your fingers . . .)

Next we loco-motored into Union and visited the Illinois Railway Museum—it's the biggest one in the U.S.! Sam and I climbed aboard horse cars, trolleys, and cabooses. You can see some of the trains in movies like <u>The Babe</u> and <u>A League of Their Own</u>, a story about the Rockford Peaches, one of America's first all-girl baseball teams.

Monkeying around,
Mia

On the eighth day of Christmas,
my cousin gave to me . . .

8 train cars
chugging

7 s'mores a-melting, 6 roadside giants, 5 golden deer,
4 soaring birds, 3 gray ghosts, 2 voyagers,
and a cardinal in a white oak tree.

Hey, Mom and Dad,

What do you give a cockatoo for his birthday? Ruby told me, but I don't speak bird.

Cookie, a Major Mitchell's cockatoo, is the oldest resident at Brookfield Zoo, right outside of Chicago. He is the only member left from the zoo's opening—over 70 years ago! Now "retired," Cookie hangs out in his keeper's office. But on his big day, he makes a special appearance. Visitors sing "Happy Birthday," and Cookie gets a muffin-sized cake.

You know I go nuts for penguins, so we waddled over to The Living Coast exhibit. Playing inside were Humboldt penguins that actually live in the desert!

Since Sam _loves_ bears, we stopped by Brookfield's largest exhibit, Great Bear Wilderness. The polar bears were chillin' in their pool, until I pressed my nose against the viewing glass. One bear swam up and—SMOOCH!—gave me an Eskimo kiss! A bear cub was the first animal bought for Chicago's Lincoln Park Zoo. For only $10! But the cub liked climbing out of his pen (and probably giving the security guards a major FREAK-OUT).

Busy cub in Illinois,
Mia

On the ninth day of Christmas,
my cousin gave to me . . .

9 penguins
playing

8 train cars chugging, 7 s'mores a-melting, 6 roadside giants,
5 golden deer, 4 soaring birds, 3 gray ghosts, 2 voyagers,
and a cardinal in a white oak tree.

Hey, Mom and Dad! Up here!

I'm sitting on "The Ledge" in Willis Tower—the tallest building in the United States!

Sam and I are on the 103rd floor, on a glass balcony that sticks out more than four feet beyond the Skydeck. Good thing I'm not afraid of heights! Above are birds. Below are clouds. And, across the rooftops, are four states—Illinois, Indiana, Michigan, and Wisconsin. From here, we can see them ALL.

Willis Tower (which used to be called the Sears Tower) is awesome. It has an elevator that makes your ears pop, and enough floor space for 101 football games. But my favorite part—and Ruby's—is the view. If I squint hard enough, I can see the boats sparkle on sunny Lake Michigan. They look as tiny as Christmas lights!

This is the place to perch, and I need one. I'm POOPED. Today we walked on Michigan Avenue, also called the Magnificent Mile. There are a jillion stores and very cool skyscrapers including The Tribune Tower. It's made of stones from everywhere—Egypt's pyramids, Japan's Golden Castle, and the MOON!

Love,
Mia

On the tenth day of Christmas,
my cousin gave to me . . .

10 boats a-sparkling

9 penguins playing, 8 train cars chugging,
7 s'mores a-melting, 6 roadside giants, 5 golden deer,
4 soaring birds, 3 gray ghosts, 2 voyagers,
and a cardinal in a white oak tree.

Dear Mom and Dad,

Today Sam said we were going to see monsters!
He turned on a football game, and there they were . . .
the Chicago Bears, MONSTERS of the Midway.

"Bear down!" cheered Uncle Joe. Aunt Mary says he goes wild
for Chicago's teams. He loves watching the Bulls play basketball, the
Blackhawks play hockey, and the Cubs or White Sox play baseball. But
during the Cubs-Sox battle for the annual Crosstown Cup, Uncle Joe
roots for his Cubbies. The teams are rivals. So are their fans.

Too bad the Cubs haven't won a championship in 100 years. Poor
Uncle Joe. Sam blames the Curse of the Billy Goat: At a 1945 World
Series game between the Cubs and Detroit Tigers, a Cubs fan brought his
pet goat for good luck. But the Cubs' owner turned the goat away. Big
mistake. The fan said that until a goat was allowed in the ballpark, the
Cubs wouldn't win a World Series. Ever. Again.

I asked Uncle Joe if he believed in the curse. He rubbed
his goatee and answered, "<u>Baaah</u>."

Your #1 fan,

Mia

On the eleventh day of Christmas,
my cousin gave to me . . .

11 Midway monsters

10 boats a-sparkling, 9 penguins playing, 8 train cars chugging, 7 s'mores a-melting, 6 roadside giants, 5 golden deer, 4 soaring birds, 3 gray ghosts, 2 voyagers, and a cardinal in a white oak tree.

Tickets please . . . .

Navy Pier in Chicago is one BIG fair. It has roller coasters, pirate shows, and "cheezborgers," and above everything towers a spinning Ferris wheel.

Get this—the very first Ferris wheel ever was built right here. It was 264 feet tall and held over 2,000 riders in boxes the size of train cars! Uncle Joe said it was made for the greatest fair in Chicago's history.

Back in 1893, millions of people traveled to Chicago to see the World's Fair. There were more than 60,000 exhibits, from the Mammoth Cheese to a 1,500-pound chocolate statue. (YUM!) Visitors saw things like the zipper, fizzy soda pop, and the hamburger . . . for the first time. All around them towered white buildings, much fancier than anything most people had ever seen. "The White City" especially amazed a visitor who later became very famous: author L. Frank Baum. The Emerald City in his book The Wonderful Wizard of Oz was inspired by what he saw!

Chicago architect Daniel Burnham sure had big plans when he helped build the city. I have big plans, too . . . for our next vacation!

Bring a truck when you pick me up at the bus station, okay? Dad's suitcase is stuffed, and I still have Christmas presents to pack. . . .

Love,
Mia

World's Fair Admit One

On the twelfth day of Christmas, my cousin gave to me . . .

12 rides a-racing

11 Midway monsters, 10 boats a-sparkling, 9 penguins playing,
8 train cars chugging, 7 s'mores a-melting, 6 roadside giants,
5 golden deer, 4 soaring birds, 3 gray ghosts, 2 voyagers,
and a cardinal in a white oak tree.

NAVY PIER

Illinois: The Prairie State

Capital: Springfield • **State abbreviation:** IL • **Largest city:** Chicago • **State bird:** the Northern cardinal • **State flower:** the violet • **State tree:** the white oak • **State insect:** the monarch butterfly • **State fossil:** the Tully monster • **State animal:** the white-tailed deer • **State reptile:** the Eastern painted turtle • **State snack food:** popcorn • **State motto:** "State Sovereignty, National Union" • **State song:** "Illinois, Illinois" • **State dance:** the square dance

Some Famous Illinoisians:

Jane Addams (1860–1935), born in Cedarville, was the first American woman to receive the Nobel Peace Prize. She fought hard for the rights of women, children, and workers, and co-founded Hull-House, a safe shelter where the poor were always welcome.

Walt Disney (1901–1966), born in Chicago, was the creator and voice of international icon Mickey Mouse. He founded the Walt Disney Company, which has produced such films as *A Bug's Life* and *The Little Mermaid*, and dreamed up the idea for Disneyland and Walt Disney World.

Marlee Matlin (1965–), born in Morton Grove, is an actress and author who lost her hearing as a child. Since that time, she has appeared in countless movies and TV shows and is the youngest woman to receive an Oscar® for Best Actress in a Leading Role.

Ronald Reagan (1911–2004) was born in Tampico. By the age of seven, he had lived in four Illinois towns and the city of Chicago. His first job was as a lifeguard at Lowell Park, saving 77 people from drowning. Reagan went to Eureka College, and later moved to California, where he acted in more than 50 movies. He was eventually elected governor of the state. Reagan served as the 40th president of the United States from 1981–1989.

Shel Silverstein (1930–1999), born in Chicago, was a poet, illustrator, playwright, screenwriter, and songwriter. He is the author of many celebrated children's books, including *The Giving Tree*, *A Light in the Attic*, and *Where the Sidewalk Ends*.

Oprah Winfrey (1954–) has been called the queen of daytime TV and the most powerful woman in the world. Her highly influential talk show, *The Oprah Winfrey Show*, ran for twenty-five years from Harpo Studios, her television production studio in Chicago.

To Milla and Sofia, my superior women. And to Paul, my Superman.
—G.B.

To Ellie, Rich, and George.
—J.E.

STERLING CHILDREN'S BOOKS
New York

An Imprint of Sterling Publishing
387 Park Avenue South
New York, NY 10016

STERLING CHILDREN'S BOOKS and the distinctive Sterling Children's Books logo are trademarks
of Sterling Publishing Co., Inc.

Text © 2012 by Gina Bellisario
Illustrations © 2012 by Jeffrey Ebbeler
The artwork for this book was created using acrylic paint on paper.
Designed by Elizabeth Phillips

ISBN 978-1-4027-9733-0

Library of Congress Cataloging-in-Publication Data

Bellisario, Gina.
 The twelve days of Christmas in Illinois / written by Gina Bellisario; illustrated by Jeffrey Ebbeler.
  p. cm.
 Summary: Mia writes a letter home each of the twelve days she spends exploring the state of Illinois at Christmastime, as
her cousin Sam shows her everything from the state capital, Springfield, to historic Route 66. Includes facts about Illinois.
 ISBN 978-1-4027-9733-0
 [1. Illinois--Fiction. 2. Christmas--Fiction. 3. Cousins--Fiction. 4. Letters--Fiction.] I. Ebbeler, Jeffrey, ill. II. Title.
 PZ7.B41466Twe 2012
 [Fic]--dc23
                          2011040861

Distributed in Canada by Sterling Publishing
c/o Canadian Manda Group, 165 Dufferin Street
Toronto, Ontario, Canada M6K 3H6
Distributed in the United Kingdom by GMC Distribution Services
Castle Place, 166 High Street, Lewes, East Sussex, England BN7 1XU
Distributed in Australia by Capricorn Link (Australia) Pty. Ltd.
P.O. Box 704, Windsor, NSW 2756, Australia

Printed in China

Lot#:
2 4 6 8 10 9 7 5 3 1
07/12

For information about custom editions, special sales and premium and corporate purchases,
please contact Sterling Special Sales at 800-805-5489 or specialsales@sterlingpublishing.com.

CRACKER JACK® is a registered trademark of Frito-Lay North America, Inc.
JUICY FRUIT® is a registered trademark of Wm. Wrigley Jr. Company.

www.sterlingpublishing.com/kids